ESCALATE
RETRIBUTION

ESCALATE
RETRIBUTION

SIGMUND BROUWER

ORCA BOOK PUBLISHERS

Library and Archives Canada Cataloguing in Publication

Brouwer, Sigmund, 1959-, author
Escalate / Sigmund Brouwer.
(Retribution)

Issued in print and electronic formats.
ISBN 978-1-4598-1484-4 (SOFTCOVER).—ISBN 978-1-4598-1485-1 (PDF).—
ISBN 978-1-4598-1486-8 (EPUB)

I. Title.
PS8553.R68467E83 2018   jc813'.54   C2017-904536-9
                             C2017-904537-7

First published in the United States, 2018
Library of Congress Control Number: 2017949690

Summary: In this installment of the high-interest Retribution series for
teen readers, Jace tracks down his birth family.

MIX
Paper from
responsible sources
FSC® C016245

*Orca Book Publishers is dedicated to preserving the environment and has
printed this book on Forest Stewardship Council® certified paper.*

Orca Book Publishers gratefully acknowledges the support for its publishing
programs provided by the following agencies: the Government of Canada
through the Canada Book Fund and the Canada Council for the Arts,
and the Province of British Columbia through the BC Arts Council
and the Book Publishing Tax Credit.

Edited by Tanya Trafford
Cover image by iStock.com
Author photo by Curtis Comeau

ORCA BOOK PUBLISHERS
www.orcabook.com

Printed and bound in Canada.

21 20 19 18 • 4 3 2 1

To Katherine Oviatt,
for all the lives you've changed for the better
through your love of sharing literacy

es·ca·late (\ˈe-skə-ˌlāt)
verb
to increase in extent, volume, number, amount, intensity or scope

ONE

Victor Lang was in eighth grade—the highest grade at M.T. Matthews, a middle school in the posh area of West Vancouver. You would think someone his age would be able to figure out that the smallest of the three kids in front of him was about to hand Victor his butt on a plate. As in beat the snot out of him.

The names of the other three? I didn't know and I didn't care. Of immediate importance was the smallest kid's stance and balance and body language. He was a full head shorter than Victor, but I could see Victor was in trouble.

It was a sunny afternoon, and they were in the shade of an elm in the park across the street from the school. From where I sat, it was obvious to me that the kid's shoulders showed tension, and his fists had formed into tight balls of solid bone. As clearly as a pitcher going into windup, he was prepping himself to throw a punch.

For the smaller kid's sake, I hoped he'd go for Victor's softer body mass. Translated, a punch in the gut. If the kid smacked Victor's cheekbone or skull, he'd probably break a finger or two.

Best thing, if you want to hurt someone, is to use your elbow. Less damage to you. More to them. I'm aware of this because part of my skill set is hurting people.

I box. I'm good at it. I only punch if I'm in the ring, with gloves to protect my hands. Outside the ring, I believe anything goes—the dirtier you fight, the better your chance of winning.

This impending punch should have been as obvious to Victor as it was to me.

Two key words—*should have.*

I knew a lot about Victor. I knew, for example, that when it came to street smarts, Victor had none.

Zero.

It wasn't that he was stupid. Victor's school records showed that his IQ was off the charts. He got straight A's in all his subjects. But book smarts are not the same as street smarts.

I knew Victor's middle name— Stephen, *ph* not *v*. I knew his age, right down to the hour and minute he was born. I knew in which room in which hospital he had taken his first squalling breaths of air. After a breach delivery at 2:32 in the morning.

I knew Victor's home address. I knew where his mom worked, her credit rating and how much she weighed. I knew that she did not carry mutated growth hormone receptor, or GHR, genes.

I knew about Elias, Victor's older brother—exactly my age—who had disappeared six months earlier.

I knew about his sister Jennie—middle child, dark hair, sixteen and the kind of girl who knew how to get her way.

I knew Victor's blood type. It was the same as mine. We both carried the A and B markers, along with the Rh factor: AB Positive. It's that boxing thing again. I'm familiar with blood. I've had my own blood smeared against an opponent's gloves, and I've had a bigger share of my opponent's blood splashed onto my own bare skin.

If I were to write it all down, I would have at least twenty pages of information about Victor Stephen Lang. Because I'd been stalking him, both in person and in cyberspace, for nearly a month.

Two more things I could add to those pages.

One, Victor deserved what he was too stupid to see coming.

Two, Victor was a bully who was about to get some payback.

And I was going to sit back and watch that first punch connect.

Even though I was almost certain that Victor Stephen Lang was my brother.

TWO

Five minutes later I crouched beside Victor. He sat knees to chin, arms around knees, head bowed.

I tapped his shoulder, and he lifted his head. "Leave me alone."

He was blubbering, a mix of tears, snot and blood dribbling onto his upper lip.

It hadn't been a gut shot like I thought it would be, but a good pop to the nose. Just a single punch. I had decided I would step in if the other two joined in or if the smaller kid kept punching, but that had not been necessary.

Victor had reacted to the punch by dropping to the ground and flailing around like a turtle on its back. Except turtles don't bawl like a baby pulled away from mommy. I'd seen the contempt on the faces of all three kids before they'd walked away.

When I didn't move, he said it again, with more attitude. "Leave me alone."

"Can't," I said. "You sent for me."

I had parted my hair neatly on the left side and slicked the bulk of it sideways with heavy-duty gel. I wore a pair of nerd glasses. I had a pen protector in the chest pocket of my shirt. My blue corduroy pants were too tight and an inch too short, showing off thick wool work socks. It was so over the top that nobody in the world should have seen it as anything more than a terrible Halloween costume.

Victor studied me and lifted a lip in scorn.

"Geek like you?" He sniffed, finding composure in a chance to belittle me.

"Hardly. I don't need my computer repaired."

I had discovered that when I dressed like this, I was invisible. I'd even conducted an experiment at Starbucks. Three in the afternoon, things slow, I ordered an Americano and gave the name Bill. Girl behind the counter smiled at me, letting the smile linger. While the coffee was being made I went into the restroom, slicked my hair back and quickly changed into geek mode. With the first coffee on the counter waiting for Bill to pick up, I ordered a hot chocolate from the same girl, watching her eyes to see if she'd recognize me. Nothing. No lingering smile either. Geeks might rule the world, but good luck on the dance floor.

Victor, nose still dripping, lifted his cell phone, waited for his thumbprint to register, then tapped a number. Without looking up, he said, "Go. Away."

I took the phone from his hand and touched the screen to stop the call.

I glanced at the contact information. It had been stored in Favorites.

"Think running to your principal for the fifth time this month is going to solve this for you?" I asked. "She did nothing for you the other times."

"My next call is the police," Victor said, holding out his hand for the phone. "Then a lawyer. Punching me was the stupidest thing he could have done. Don't they know that *anti-bullying* is a hot buzzword? The trouble those three just got into is—"

Victor stopped. "Wait a minute. You said *fifth time this month*. How did you know?"

Took him long enough.

"You sent for me," I repeated. "The message said nobody was helping you and that your life was miserable."

It took him another moment.

"You?" He snorted with disbelief. "Part of the so-called shadowy legend? As in *When those in power have turned on you,*

you can turn to us for help? Sorry, man, didn't realize you were actually Team Joke, not Team Retribution. I thought it was a boxer and a hacker and a climber babe and a pickpocket artist who could be a supermodel."

My brother Bentley was the hacker. Raven climbed buildings. Jo often disguised herself as a boy. Pickpocketing was a strength but it was in forgery that she really excelled. And I punched people.

"What, I don't look like a hacker?" I said. I had an infinity tattoo on my right shoulder. A team symbol. But I didn't really like to think of us as a team. More like independent contractors who traded favors. Reluctantly.

"Hacker would always be behind a computer or carrying a laptop," he said. "So if you are a hacker, you're not a good one, and I'm not interested. What I want is someone with some muscle."

He pulled a tissue from his pocket. And he thought I was the geek? Who in eighth grade walked around with tissues? Really.

He blew his nose and tossed the tissue to the ground.

"Not a fan of litter," I said. I took two pens from my pocket protector and used them like chopsticks to pick up the tissue and shove it into the pocket protector. The pens I put in my back pants pocket.

"If I throw a stick," Victor said, "will you chase it and leave?"

Some forms of bullying were not physical. Victor, I'd learned, was an expert.

"Victor," I said, "we get a lot of messages. When we show up to help, you shouldn't take it lightly."

The rumors about a hidden forum on the Internet were true. Brother Bentley handled the incoming pleas for help.

"You were five minutes too late," Victor said. "What I need is a team of full-time bodyguards, not a pencil neck like you who bounced off every branch of the ugly tree on the way down."

"That's not how it works," I told him. "If you really want help, you might want to listen instead of practicing your insults. Although clearly you need the practice. Ugly tree? Not original. Or funny."

Truth was, his problem didn't qualify at all for help from the Retribution crew. I'd kept this mission to myself. To learn what I'd learned about Victor, I'd had to lie to my brother.

"I fart in your general direction," Victor said. "Your mother was a hamster, and your father—"

"Smelled of elderberries," I finished for him. "Not original either. From *Monty Python and the Holy Grail*. And last Tuesday you used it to make a boy in third grade cry. "

"I'm trying to picture you with duct tape across your mouth," Victor said. "It's a pleasant daydream. Now give me my phone."

My own phone vibrated. **Bat Cave. One hour.**

It was a message from Bentley. With traffic, it would take me a half hour to get there. Maybe longer. I'd want time to clean up first, so factor in a shower too.

This conversation was over anyway. I handed Victor his phone and walked away.

I really did not like this guy. But while things hadn't gone as expected, I wasn't walking away without something for my efforts.

Proof of whether I would be forever stuck with him as a brother was crumpled up in my plastic pocket protector.

THREE

"Bat Cave" was the term Bentley mockingly used for the place where we'd grown up as brothers and still shared. While I knew full well what Bentley was implying, on three levels he was wrong, and Bentley is rarely wrong.

First, in the caped crusader's universe, it's known as the Batcave. One word. Not two. In the original comic it began as a secret tunnel between Batman's Wayne Manor and an old barn where he kept the Batmobile. Then, when later writers transformed the simple tunnel into a labyrinth with crime lab and workshop, they called it "The Bat's Cave." Eventually that morphed into Batcave, the newly created noun, I suppose, giving it an air of importance.

Second, the place where Bentley and I live is not cave-like at all. Do a Google image search for "Vancouver mansions," and ours will pop up in the first ten. Hint: it's the biggest one. Our family owns more of similar size across the world. And we don't fly commercial to get to those places.

Third, in case it wasn't obvious by my referring to it as the place where Bentley and I grew up, it's not home.

Recently, much to my satisfaction, our father had been arrested for a sensational front-page-news type of crime, and the reverberations at our family mansion had yet to die down. Given the tissue in my pocket, loaded with DNA to test, I expected the aftershocks of his crime were about to go seismic again.

Let's get this straight. I'm not proud in any sense to be part of this mansion. In the weeks right after my father's arrest, I spent some time living on the streets, trying to make sense of how life had turned for me. I was only back at that mansion because Bentley had begged me. Our mother is a largely absent figure anyway, and he said he was miserable without a brother around.

Again, given the tissue I had on me, Bentley's declaration was a stab in the heart.

So yeah, I was dealing with some crap in my life, long-term and short-term.

I didn't need a therapist to tell me that I fight some deep-rooted insecurities over the fact that tuition at the private school I attend costs per year what is considered a good level of middle income. While I've dumped the Ferrari for a black suv with tinted windows to make it tougher for media to snap photos, the Ferrari is still parked in one of the garages. Next to a Lamborghini.

And I literally fight those insecurities. Just about every night I park my SUV blocks from a boxing gym so nobody will guess where I came from. I prove myself in the ring, where no amount of money proves whether a person has heart or toughness.

On that level, Bentley's reference to the Batcave was bang on. Rich boy living a secret identity, fighting crime. That was me, I suppose. Jace Wyatt as a watered-down version of Bruce Wayne. Maybe reading Batman comics as a kid *had* influenced my subconscious.

That, in essence, was the long-term crap of my life.

The short-term was walking into the room in the mansion where Bentley had set up his bank of computers and having to put on a brave face and pretend I was not living with a secret that would devastate him.

Bad enough I had to pretend cheerfulness. Batman, at least, didn't have to deal with a couple of femme fatales named Raven and Jo, who were clearly waiting to pounce.

Made me glad I'd first showered the gel out of my hair and changed out of my geek clothes. Because showing up as Johnny Nerd would have led to questions I wasn't prepared to answer.

FOUR

"Hope you're on the card later tonight for women's wrestling," I said to the two of them. "Otherwise, that would be a complete waste of makeup."

In my street life I made money playing speed chess with pigeons disguised as tourists. My entrance line was the equivalent of moving a white pawn to E4 as a game opener. Because with Raven and Jo the best strategy was something like the Sicilian Dragon. Direct offense. Something you should never do unless you're prepared for continued carnage on both sides of the board.

"Better bring up your translating app," Jo said to Raven. Jo's mixed heritage gave her an amazing exotic vibe that always took me a substantial amount of effort to ignore. "He's speaking idiot already."

Bentley swung his head from Jo to Raven. She was dark-haired and intense— no surprise, given her name.

"Jo," Raven said. "That's so totally not appropriate. Look at Jace. Wonderful. Intelligent. So clearly filled with love for all humans." She paused. "Oh, wait. The lying competition is tomorrow night."

"I need to up my meds," I said. "Maybe that way something you say will strike me as funny."

"Or," Jo said, "maybe it's time to—"

"Time to talk about the reason we're here tonight," Bentley said.

Apparently he wasn't enjoying our witty banter.

He pushed his swivel chair away from his desk. Bentley loved that swivel chair.

Gave him a chance to spin in circles without effort.

His feet didn't get in the way because they didn't reach the floor.

Bentley was born with a recessive-gene thing. Both parents have to have the dormant recessive gene, and both have to pass along the recessive gene. Mom passes it down and Dad doesn't, you're okay. Dad passes it down and Mom doesn't, you're okay. One in four chance, then, that the throw of the dice at conception lands with both passing it down. When that happens, you're insensitive to your body's growth hormones. Short version of the explanation, you're short and you stay short. Along with that comes a prominent forehead and a pushed-in nasal bridge.

It's called Laron syndrome. Dwarfism. Bentley did his own fighting, but from behind computer monitors that literally and metaphorically hid him from the world. Not difficult to guess what a therapist would make of that.

"At least you didn't text out *Code Red*," Raven said, pretending it had never been her idea to use it in the first place.

"Be okay to get rid of the whole Batcave thing too," Jo said to Bentley. "Or was that an unoriginal fantasy belonging to your Diva Boy brother?"

I opened my mouth to fire back, but Bentley jumped in again.

"Let's stick to business," he said, turning to me. "Bro, we haven't seen a lot of you lately. Got a private project happening? Anything we can help you with?"

I shook my head. It just hurt, knowing how much Bentley trusted me.

"It can't be work that's taking Jace away from us," Jo said. "Unless primping in front of a mirror counts as work."

"Well then," I snapped back, "clearly you're unemployed."

"Hey," Jo said. "That's dangerously close to body shaming."

"Also," Raven said, "contradicts your first statement about our makeup."

She grinned. So did Jo. I was no match for them.

"If I had a gavel, I'd be banging the table," Bentley said. "I wanted you to watch something that came to us via the forum."

As in chat-room forums. Bentley monitored the Internet for any discussions that involved Team Retribution.

"It was a video request," he said. "I think it's worth getting involved. But it might drag us into the corporate world, which, sadly, is still biased toward males with nice threads and flashy watches. My vote is Jace fronts it. He's used to sparring with lawyers and bean counters."

"Guess being a trust-fund kid is good for something," Raven said.

"Happy to let him deal with that crap," Jo said. "Roll the video."

Bentley flipped a screen around. His fingers raced on the keyboard, and he brought up a link.

A girl's face filled the screen. Okay, not quite a girl. My age. Long blond hair. Big blue eyes. Tears trickling down her cheeks.

And very, very attractive.

"My name is Deanna Steele," she began. "I don't know who else I can turn to for help."

Going suit-and-tie was a sacrifice I would have to make, I told myself. If we were the only ones left to turn to, what choice did I have?

FIVE

Deanna Steele's choice of meeting place was a Tim Hortons. The next afternoon I did the standard recon thing and showed up a half hour early. We had already earned ourselves some enemies. Sooner or later we'd show up to help someone and find it was a trap.

Timmies is a great place to watch for watchers. Traffic flow is constant. Anyone sitting alone for more than half an hour is going to stick out. It's easy enough to look occupied by propping a newspaper or device in front of you. Not so easy to hide the telltale signs of scanning the room instead of giving your reading material your full attention.

Of course, the same went for me. I didn't have a prop to fake-read. I sat in a booth, openly glancing around. But I wanted any watcher to know that I was watching.

There was an elderly man—and by that I mean over the age of fifty and balding—who kept looking around as his coffee cooled and glancing at his watch. I was prepared to believe he was waiting for someone to join him, but I'd also make sure he didn't follow me out of the coffee shop. I'd already been burned by an investigator who'd betrayed me to my father. Fool me once, shame on you. But twice? You know how the saying goes.

Deanna Steele showed up exactly on time. It would have been hard to miss her. She drove a Porsche 718 Boxster— the snappy two-seater that starts at about $65,000 US. It was cherry red. I'd watched her circle the parking lot four times, even though there were plenty of spots available. She eventually parked right in front of the main window and took her time getting to the door. This was a blue-collar part of town. Lots of the men around me were grizzled, wearing work boots and paint-splattered coveralls. They definitely noticed her entrance. Even if there had been a grease fire in the kitchen, she would have been the focal point.

She sashayed—love that word, *sash-ayed*—through the doors like she was inspecting the franchise as a possible purchase. She sported designer clothes, designer purse and designer white teeth, obviously the result of expensive braces and diligent bleaching.

Good thing I'd been given this task. With this girl's focus on outward appearances, Jo or Raven would have been inclined to tear her apart and leave pieces of her carcass in the sun to dry to wrinkled leather. They'd do the same to a guy who loved to pose.

Me, on the other hand? While I wasn't impressed by the show of wealth—my mom is sitting on a half billion dollars of generations-old wealth—I did admire her brazenness. This, I thought, might be fun.

She surveyed the room and caught my eye. I was geeked out again, right down to the slicked-sideways hair. I wasn't worried about her recognizing me as Jace Wyatt, as in Jace Wyatt of the Wyatt Foundation, or Jace Wyatt, son of disgraced and recently jailed surgeon Winchester Wyatt. Her money didn't come close to traveling in the same circles as mine. I dressed this way because of some ancient Chinese military strategy I'd read about in a book called *The Art of War*: "He who exercises no forethought but makes light of his opponents is sure to be captured by them." In other words, don't underestimate your enemy. And if underestimating your enemy was a bad thing, then getting your enemy to underestimate you was a good thing. Besides, if you lower the expectations of people around you, it's much easier to live up to them.

I gave her a weak smile and waggled my fingers, guessing this would be the awestruck reaction she felt entitled to from a geek like me.

I caught a subtle waft of expensive perfume as she sat down across from me.

"Infinite," she said.

"Possibilities," I answered. A little code thing that Bentley had set up for her.

"Chai tea," she said. "Two milk, two sweetener. And a straw. So I don't stain my teeth when I drink."

This wasn't part of the code thing. Probably more of a test on her part. Or maybe she just expected everyone to be happy to serve her. So. Would I drool and leap at the chance?

I drooled and I leapt.

Yeah, I thought. This was definitely going to be fun.

SIX

"Tell me about the team," Deanna said. She lifted her chai tea with straw to her lips. Careful not to smear her bright-red lipstick, she nibbled on the straw to draw a sip. "It sounds so cool and mysterious."

Team? No. I did my thing. Raven and Jo did theirs. We traded help and favors. That was all. Bentley was probably the only one who liked thinking of us as a team.

"What I think is cool," I answered, "is that it only feels like you pull liquid upward through a straw. What really happens is that after you suck air out of the straw, atmospheric pressure *pushes* the liquid down to fill the vacuum. We're close to sea level, which means there's about sixty miles of air pushing down on us, so it's about fourteen pounds per square inch, more than enough to force the tea upward. I mean, commercial jets fly based on a lift of only a few pounds per square inch across the wings."

I expected her to dismiss my geek comment, which was why I had thrown it out there. As a simple distraction. I didn't want to reveal information about Jo or Raven or Bentley. Instead, she tilted her head and gave it some thought.

"Huh," she said. "But if all that atmosphere can push tea up the straw, why don't I feel like I'm being crushed?"

"We're made of bone and water," I said. "Percentage varies by gender. So you're roughly 50 percent skeleton and 50 percent liquid. Fourteen pounds per inch isn't nearly enough to crush water or bone."

"Huh," she said again. She gave me a full and frank gaze. Her blue eyes were enhanced by masterfully applied makeup. "Clearly you are the brains of the team. I like that."

I gave her the bashful grin that any geek would give when patted on the head like a puppy.

After another sip Deanna said, "I hear the two girls on the team are kick-ass. And hot."

"Well…"

"And there's the fighter, right?"

"Boxer," I said. Fighting is crude. Boxing takes strategy and discipline. Bloody results might be the same, but still…

"He kind of has a Johnny Depp vibe going on, is what the rumors say. When Depp was young and before he got all seedy-looking, I mean."

"That's fairly accurate," I said. "Some people say he has the ability to make Depp look like a geek in comparison."

She sighed. "I'd like to meet the boxer. Was hoping he'd be here. No insult or anything."

I gave her a wounded but brave smile. Depp wasn't the only one who could act.

"Don't get me wrong," she said. "Intelligence has a good vibe too. Different but good."

I got the implication. She was establishing early that I'd been placed in the friend zone. Forever.

"So," I said. "Someone is blackmailing you?"

She dug out her device, swiped the screen, found what she needed and handed it to me. "Link to a private YouTube video. Only I can access it."

I tapped the screen to play. A series of photos came up, taken, I guessed, by a drone. A few photos of a man and a woman, casually dressed, sitting in lounge chairs beside a swimming pool, enjoying the sun and glasses of wine. Then a couple of photos where the woman was leaning over the man, kissing him. Nothing that couldn't be printed in a daily newspaper.

"Must be something high at stake here. We're not talking tens of thousands of dollars, are we? It's more, right?"

She blinked. "Hundreds of thousands. You guessed that just from the photos?"

"The technology involved is expensive," I said. "Nobody would go to that much trouble to take those photos unless it was worth it."

"Technology?"

"Private link. No point in putting photos online of something that looks like an innocent kiss between consenting adults. Means either the man isn't supposed to be kissing the woman or the woman isn't supposed to be kissing the man. Which means if they knew there was a drone above, they'd make sure not to be caught like they were. The drone was too high to be seen or heard. Expensive technology. And close-up, high-def photos from that altitude means an expensive camera and a skilled operator."

I handed her back the device.

"The man in the picture is my father," she said. Flat voice. "And the woman is his secretary. So no, not innocent at all."

"Hurts?" I asked.

"Yes," she said. "I'm trying not to hate him. And yet I have no choice but to protect him."

Suddenly, with her pain so raw and obvious, this wasn't fun anymore.

"Tell me more," I said. Quietly.

"Huh," she said.

"Huh?"

She studied my face. "Interesting accidental shift there. Like suddenly you're a real person."

She touched the roughness of my knuckles, hardened by hours of punching the heavy bag in the gym. "These aren't computer hands."

I didn't move.

She reached over and pulled off my glasses. She removed the plastic pocket protector from my shirt pocket. She half stood and leaned over and ran her fingers through my hair, roughing it up.

She sat back again and examined me as she wiped her hands on a napkin to get my hair goop off her fingers.

"Roll up your sleeves," she said.

This was the voice of a new Deanna Steele. Tougher than the one who didn't want to stain her teeth by drinking chai tea without a straw.

I saw no point in not obeying her. I'm not muscled like a steroid user. But hitting a speed bag for hundreds of hours definitely adds some definition to your forearms and biceps.

She took her time evaluating my arms before speaking again. "So you're the mysterious Johnny Depp one. For the record, though, he kicks your butt as an actor. In fact, even I'm better than you.

Totally bought into the entitled-princess act, didn't you?"

My mind was flicking through what this meant. In short, she'd been the one to get me to underestimate her.

She pulled the straw from her chai tea and drank directly from the cup, leaving a lipstick stain on the edge.

"How about we start over?" she said. "No pretending on either side. Geek and princess are no longer at the table."

"Sounds good," I said. She'd won the first round, but I wasn't going down without more of a fight. "You owe me a beverage. I'll take a coffee. One cream."

She arched an eyebrow.

"Please?" I said, defeated again.

"I would be happy to get it for you," she said, rising to go stand in line.

Not going to lie. I watched her walk away and enjoyed the view. Now it was back to fun again.

SEVEN

My device buzzed, showing a 416 area code. Toronto. I'd been expecting the call. Noon here in Vancouver, three PM there.

It wasn't the most convenient time to take a call. Victor Lang was facing another beating, and this time it looked like I had no choice but to step in.

It was Saturday, and I was back in my geek disguise in the park opposite M.T. Matthews school, watching Victor Lang sitting alone reading comic books. Just as five high-school kids walked up to him, I'd been thinking about the unfortunate

choice of initials for a school. M.T.—
empty. Empty Matthews school?

Even though I should have been
thinking about the blackmailing problem
that Deanna Steele had shared with me
the afternoon before at Timmies, Empty
Matthews school had led my brain down
a very juvenile path of silly book titles
and authors. *Rusty Bedsprings*, by I.P.
Nightly, and the sequel, *Down the Yellow
River*, by I.P. Dailey. *All Alone*, by Saul
E. Terry. *Allegiance to the King*, by Neil
Down.

I knew dozens of similar titles and
names because when we were younger,
Bentley would sneak into my bedroom
late at night when he was scared or
lonely, which was basically every night.
When I'd discovered that he giggled like
crazy over these kinds of silly titles and
author names, I'd make sure to have two
or three new ones each night to distract
him. Then he'd started finding ones to

bring to me, and it had become another way to bond as brothers.

Athletic Supporter, by Jacques Strap. *Credit Cards*, by Bill Melater. And our all-time favorite, *Big Fart*, by Hugh Jass. Bentley had laughed so hard telling me that one, he'd fallen on his back and kicked his legs in the air, repeating it five or six times more. He was ten.

One of my favorite memories. And that one, like all the others I could flip through like a photo album, could be destroyed by this incoming call.

My phone rang as I stood up from the bench and began walking toward Victor and the five bigger boys surrounding him. They were clearly high-school age like me. Looked like jocks with a sheen of nastiness to them. It's what traveling in packs tended to do to humans oozing testosterone.

"Jace Wyatt," I said. "Yes. And the password is: 'infinite possibilities.' Is it a match?"

I just wanted a yes or a no. I had no time for pleasantries, not with the aggression I could see rising in the nasty jocks gathered around Victor.

The woman on the other end confirmed my identity and began the preamble about test results and the mathematical odds that made it impossible for them to be wrong on a paternity test.

Ahead of me, two kids, one on either side of Victor, had grabbed his arms.

"I'm sorry. I realize this will sound rude," I said, interrupting, "but I'm in the middle of an urgent situation. I can call back later for more details. What I'd like right now is for you to give me a *yes, it's positive*, or a *no, it's not*."

She gave me the answer.

I hit *End* and slipped the device back into my pocket.

I broke into a run. Victor was about to take the first of what looked like a flurry of punches.

EIGHT

Some might argue that it had been wrong of me to remain on the sidelines a couple of days earlier when the smaller kid popped Victor in the nose. I get that. Here's my defense. I'd seen enough to know that Victor had, over a period of time, relentlessly bullied that kid verbally. I mean, I'd gotten a taste of it myself when I wandered over after the event.

The problem was, Victor didn't appear to have a good sense of self-confidence or self-respect. He lashed out at everyone else to build himself up. What I'd hoped was that by letting the two of them sort it out, Victor would realize that actions had consequences. And maybe they'd even gain a little respect for each other.

Good intentions. Bad result.

Especially if the current situation was any indication.

I arrived at the outer circle just as I heard the ringleader say, "Dude. You are absolutely the jerk who spray-painted our cars. Got it on video. You should be thanking us for this. We didn't call the cops."

I groaned.

It drew their attention. Football players, I guessed. Crew cuts giving them the blocky-headed look of linebackers, matching the squareness of their shoulders.

I ignored the collective hostility of the five jocks.

"Seriously?" I said, speaking to Victor. "Spray paint? Their cars?"

"Geek boy," the ringleader said. "Might want to stay out of this."

He had a wispy beard. Young face. Adult body. And some serious rage.

"I understand the anger," I replied to Wispy Beard. "What's the damage, you think?"

"Their cars were pieces of crap," Victor said. "They should pay me for hiding the rust spots."

"Guys," I said, stepping between them and Victor, "I'd like to hit him myself. Trust me."

Wispy Beard snorted. "Be like someone threw a marshmallow at him."

The others laughed. Apparently Wispy Beard spoke for all of them.

"I mean it," I said. "All told, what was the damage? I know about this place online. Sort of like a public trust fund to help people who have been vandalized. I could fill out the forms for you, make sure you got the money within a week."

At that moment I had a flash of how difficult it must be to be a parent. The public fund didn't exist. It would come from my generous monthly allowance, which I rarely spent through anyhow. But if I stepped in and covered for Victor, how would he ever learn? Maybe I should set up a plan for him to pay me back. What kind of stupid, attention-seeking move was that anyway, getting caught spray-painting cars at a high school?

Yes, what Victor Lang needed was tough love. Just not right now. Five high-school kids against a middle-school kid was unfair. So, I told myself, in this moment I was protecting the concept of fairness. Not enabling Victor and his obvious lack of social smarts.

"I love sucking pimples," Wispy Beard said.

I cocked my head. So far the other four weren't closing in on me. They would wait for Wispy Beard to give them the nod.

"Each to his own and all that," I said, incredulous. "I mean, it's not illegal, so who am I to judge? But seriously, people actually let you suck their pimples?"

Wispy Beard's face flushed, the taut skin on his cheekbones tinged with white. "That's what he spray-painted on my car. Those words. *I love sucking pimples.*"

I glanced at Victor and shook my head. "Really? Really?"

"I had to use little words that these morons would understand," said Victor.

"And you know they are right here, listening to every word you say."

"I used the word *moron* because it's highly unlikely it's in their vocabularies," Victor said. "We should be good."

Wispy Beard thumped himself on the chest. Like a gorilla.

"Listen, guy, I'm as mad at him as you are," I said. "But five of you, all bigger than him? There's nothing fair about this fight."

"It's not supposed to be fair, or even be a fight," Wispy Beard said. "It's supposed to be punishment."

The skinniest of the five stepped toward me. Not that he was skinny in any sense. He must have outweighed me by forty pounds.

"Can you think of a better way?" Skinny Guy asked me. "Let the cops handle it and have us in court arguing that we *don't* love to suck pimples?"

I turned to Victor. "Why would you do this?"

"To force Team Retribution to send in the bodyguards," he answered. "Any moron could understand the brilliance of this. But maybe you're not even qualified to be a moron. Looks like you're going to have to take a beating. Maybe *then* the bodyguards will show up."

I let out a heavy, heavy sigh. For Victor's stupidity. And for the fact that

I seemed to be down to two choices—let them beat him up, or stop them.

"They're not going to beat me up," I said.

"Good thinking," Wispy Beard said. "We'll let you slide on this one. Get gone."

I locked my fingers and placed both hands on top of my head, palms down.

"What I meant," I said to Victor, "is that if they don't walk, I'm not going to let them beat you up. Painful as it is to help you out of this hole you dug."

"Try not to bleed on me when they're finished with you," Victor said.

Could the kid be any more obnoxious?

I swiveled toward Wispy Beard, palms still on the top of my head, and said, "Bring it. You and me. I leave my hands on my head. You win, I walk away and he is all yours. I win—no hands—all of you walk away. Deal?"

I'd been hoping a direct challenge to him would make the others back off.

I was wrong.

NINE

Two of the goons stepped up and grabbed me by my biceps, keeping my elbows stationary. I kept my hands on my head, knowing it made my position look weaker.

First mistake—I could still move my forearms by releasing my locked fingers.

"Make him puke first," the guy on my right elbow said. "Remember what happened last time when you broke the guy's nose first and made him puke after? He almost suffocated."

Second mistake. Now I knew how the attack would unfold. Punch to the gut, punch to the nose.

"Please don't," I said. "No one is going to like how this ends."

Wispy Beard grinned. "You're half right. You won't like how it ends."

He stepped in. I was watching to see how much hip and shoulder turn he'd throw into his punch. With the proper technique, a big guy like him could turn his fist into a spear.

My guess was that he'd been using his bulk to intimidate people for years and had never had any need to learn how to throw a good punch. My guess was correct.

The punch was long and lazy, something I could have sidestepped with my legs wrapped together by duct tape. I could see it would be mainly arm, with no turning of hips and shoulders to add power, so deciding not to slip the punch wasn't much of a gamble.

I tensed my abdominal muscles and waited for the blow. I do three hundred crunches a day, so when the muscles are tight, it's a decently solid wall. The difficult part was holding back a grunt at impact. That would have spoiled much of the effect.

He'd expected me to try to double over from pain and start puking.

Instead I gave him a calm smile.

As intended, it rattled him. Now he was wondering who I was.

"Last chance," I told him, hands still on my head. His punch had stung pretty hard. It took a bit of effort to speak normally. "No one is going to like how this ends."

His answer was to throw the next punch—the nose breaker—a move as predictable as a sunrise. And as slow to unfold.

I unlocked my fingers and swung both hands from my head toward the front of my chest. That took little effort. The guys on each side of me were holding my biceps and allowing my elbows to serve nicely as stabilizing points.

I used the downward momentum of my right hand to hit the inside of his forearm and deflect his punch away from my face. His punch slid past my ribs, grazing my shirt.

His own momentum brought him forward and off-balance, close enough for me to lightly slap his face with my left hand.

It wasn't meant to be much more than a tap. But it did the job as a distraction.

His eyes opened wide, his focus on my hand.

That's when I brought my knee up with as much force as possible, making direct contact in the center of his groin. He doubled over, falling into the guy holding my left bicep.

That, in turn, was enough of a distraction to allow me to yank my left elbow loose and pivot hard to my right. The guy holding the other bicep was locked into place, and I brought my knee up again.

Same result.

I swung back to my left and spent two seconds pretending the guy's face was a speed bag. I pulled my punches as I hit him with a succession of jabs. I did not want to injure my fingers. I didn't want to hurt him too badly either.

Two guys now doubled over. A third guy in shock. Two other guys uninjured but hanging back, slack-jawed in disbelief.

And Victor, drawing out one word in admiration. "Dude!"

"We stop right now," I told the jocks. "Two of you can help carry the other three away. And I'll make sure damages are covered on your cars. We don't stop, you'll each be going down, one at a time, until there's nobody left to help carry any of you away. And no money to cover the damages." I paused to let my words sink in. "Stop? Or continue?"

They were backing away. I took that as a sign that the choice was to stop.

"Get your contact information to Victor here," I said. "You'll see your money in about a week. Try to hurt him again and I'll hunt you down. Are we clear?"

I waited for one of them to nod. Wispy Beard finally did, eyes on the ground.

"Thanks," I said.

I looked at Victor. "And you. Five hours a week of community service at a place of my choice for the next eight weeks. That will cover the damages. You good with that?"

He gulped and nodded.

It was okay to wish we were in a world where people could talk things out. But since we weren't, it wasn't a bad thing to be good at the alternative.

TEN

"Deanna Steele," I began, wincing as I shifted in the booth across from Jo and Raven, "wants us to commit a crime."

We were at a window booth in the local Denny's. Always, we agree on a window. Need to see the streets. Tonight rain misted the pavement, and the lights reflected the rainbow sheen of oil in puddles.

We also always agree that facing the door is the best place to sit. Unfortunately, three on one side of a booth is awkward.

Our compromise is simple. We take turns choosing the location of our meetings. The person who chooses the place gets to sit with their back to the door.

Tonight it was my turn. Denny's was always my pick. My entire life in the mansion had been based on pretense. I was tired of pretending and posturing. You didn't see much of either at a Denny's.

As a team—tonight, for a change, that wasn't the reason I kept wincing with pain—we'd occasionally get together because of kids we were trying to help.

Jo recently had us tracking down a friend that no one else cared about, a runaway with a history of drug abuse. She'd ended up going undercover in some fight club.

Raven had done some undercover work as well, in a shady medical clinic after we'd learned that a series of teen suicides seemed to be linked.

They both owed me more than a couple of favors.

I wasn't going to tell them about Victor Lang just yet, but in the meantime there was the Deanna Steele problem.

"Passing gas?" Raven asked.

I guess my wince was obvious. "It's just a look I get when I realize I'm stuck with you two," I answered. "Is there a tattoo for infinite pain?"

Jo grinned. "You two are so sweet. What kind of crime are we talking? Major? Minor? Deception? Full-on assault?"

"As you know from her video," I said, "it's a blackmail situation."

"But she wouldn't give details until someone met her," Jo said. "We trust she couldn't resist spilling her heart to you?"

"Nobody could," I said.

Predictably, Raven rolled her eyes. She would have been disappointed if I hadn't said that. I would have been disappointed if she hadn't rolled her eyes.

"Her father is in the middle of some kind of corporate takeover," I continued. "The blackmailer has compromising photos of her father with his secretary."

"How does Deanna know her father is being blackmailed?" Jo asked. "Seems to me he'd want to keep that quiet. That's the whole point of allowing yourself to be blackmailed."

"My bad," I said. "He's not being blackmailed. She is."

"The daughter?" Raven said. "And tell us what's going on with the weird faces. Once or twice might be your attempt at being funny, but by the fourth time, we know something's up."

"Muscle pain," I said. The fact that I had a bruise the size of a dinner plate on my abdomen was my business, not theirs. "From a boxing thing. And yes, Deanna is being blackmailed. The photos were sent to her. The blackmailers are demanding access to her father's computer or they will release the photos."

"How would photos about an illicit affair affect a corporate takeover?" Jo asked. "I mean, crappy as it is, lots of people have affairs."

"I'd be impressed if one of you could tell me what Alaska Airlines and Forever 21 and Mary Kay Cosmetics have in common," I said.

Raven said, "If I was here to impress you, I would have—"

Jo said to her, "Easy, girl."

To me, Jo said, "Airlines and clothing and makeup. We could be here all day guessing at the connection. How about you just tell us."

"High-profile companies with strong religious foundations. Alaska Airlines includes note cards with Bible verses on breakfast trays. Forever 21 puts Bible verses on the bottom of their shopping bags. And Mary Kay—"

"This matters because…" Raven said. Her photo would never appear in the dictionary beside the word *patient*.

"Some companies like that include morality clauses in their employment contracts," I answered.

"Kind of like athletes sign when they accept an endorsement deal?" Jo asked.

"Exactly," I said. "So if the photos get out, Deanna's father loses his job, and the marriage is over."

"Does the father know that the daughter knows about the photos?"

I shook my head. "Can you imagine what that must be like for her? She's mad at her dad for being unfaithful to her mom, but she feels like she has to protect him, and the way to protect him is by stealing digital data from him. He's betrayed their family, and she has to betray him in return."

For once Jo and Raven gave me sympathetic looks. I didn't kid myself.

I knew those looks were meant for Deanna, not me.

"The plan?" Raven asked.

"Easy," I said. "Identify the blackmailer, and to keep it all secret, find a way to blackmail them in return."

"Right," Jo said. "Easy."

ELEVEN

"Chances are great I won't die from cancer," said Bentley.

He spoke with a studied casualness.

"The antioxidants from vitamin C in the orange juice?" I asked. "Or the omega-3 fatty acids from our salmon?"

We were sitting in one of our family courtyards, a scene straight from a glossy architecture magazine, complete with perfect sunshine bouncing off the perfect umbrella above our glass-topped table and wrought-iron chairs. The paving stones around the infinity pool had been imported from Italy, the designer furniture from France, the freshly squeezed orange juice from Florida, and the smoked salmon on cheese from Denmark.

"You should have noted the singular in my statement, and the absence of plural. Chances are *I* won't die of cancer. Not chances are *we* won't die of cancer. While *we* are sharing the biochemical benefits of orange juice and salmon, my use of singular implies that something limited to me means my chances of dying from cancer are lower than yours. Care to guess what that might be? Hint: I'm shorter than you."

Not only was it unusual for Bentley to refer to his size, but there was also something in his tone that put me on alert. This was not our usual banter of one brother trying to out-intellect the other.

"Just got this great book out of the library," I said. "It's called *Twenty Yards to the Outhouse*."

"Written by Willie Maykit," Bentley said in an irritated voice. "Illustrated by

Betty Wont. Reviewed by Andy Dint. Why did you hire a private detective to deliver an information dump when you'd already asked me to do it?"

"I'm not going to bother to ask you how you know," I said. "I think the key point is why are you spying on me? This is just a routine missing-persons request."

"Deflection isn't going to work here, Jace," said Bentley calmly. "If you're looking for Elias Lang, I've found him for you."

I had been reaching for my glass of orange juice when he said these words. I wanted to drop my hand. I couldn't. That would reveal too much. I hoped my hand wouldn't shake as I lifted it. That would reveal more.

I managed to sip without any trembling.

"At first," Bentley said, "I was hurt. I thought you and I were a team. I thought you needed me. Going to someone else shows you don't."

I started to speak, but he waved me off.

"But your source isn't that good," Bentley said. "So at least I can retain a little pride and dignity. Your source is still looking for Elias. I'm not. I've found him. He's in a remote village in the south of Ecuador."

"You know this because…?"

"Don't try more deflection. All the other times I hack for you and Raven and Jo, you don't ask how I find it out. The methods I used matter little compared to what else I know. Like, take this for a bit of interesting trivia. Elias Lang has the exact same birthday as you. Mere coincidence, I'm sure, but still a little weird."

My body felt as if my heart had actually stopped. Was Bentley toying with me? Did he know the real reason I wanted information about the Lang family?

"And like the fact that he's in a village with a very high percentage of people with Laron syndrome," Bentley said. "A community with one hundred people just like me. Any guesses as to why he might have run away to Ecuador without telling anyone? I mean, he's your age. That's not your typical teen-runaway destination."

"He's got Laron syndrome," I said.

"Oh, so you did know that," Bentley said. "Which makes me wonder even more about your motivation to look for this Elias Lang among all the runaways out there who need to be found. Pity for the short guys? Or were you thinking it would be nice to find a matching freak for your brother so I wouldn't feel so alone in the world?"

Bentley had never referred to himself as a freak before.

"That would be so wonderful," he continued. "He and I could start a club. We have so much going for us, matching genetic defects and all."

Did Bentley also know about the

results from the DNA test done on Victor Lang's discarded tissue? I wondered if my heart would ever start beating again. I felt rigid.

"Yeah," Bentley continued. "Matching genetic defects. He and I both have parents who each carry a mutated GHR gene. As you might know, that means Elias and I were born with defective receptors in the liver that ensure our bodies can't manufacture the right growth hormones. Therefore, it's extremely unlikely that we'll ever face the runaway cell production typical of most cancers. And I know this because…"

I stayed silent. I didn't trust my voice. Plus, my stopped heart made it difficult to breathe.

"Because," he repeated, "the obscure remote village he picked as a runaway destination is a mecca for researchers trying to decipher the anti-disease properties that seem to go hand in hand with Laron syndrome. I'm sure that's how he heard about it. He's probably just hoping he can fit in there instead of trying to get around in a world like ours where people judge us for our size. I mean, now that I know about this place, I might have to visit it myself."

"Bentley…" I said.

"Nope. You don't have the right to speak about this to me. I'm not interested in making friends with some other dwarf I've never met, no matter how good your intentions were."

Blood began to flow through my veins again. He *didn't* know the real reason. The connection between Elias and Bentley was so obvious that Bentley couldn't see it.

"Okay," I said to Bentley as softly as possible. "Just let me know when you'll be ready to accept my apology."

"How about we just let this go instead?" Bentley answered. "Just go ahead and let the Lang family know where Elias is and that he's okay. I can understand you wanting to help them with that. As for the fact that he also has Laron syndrome and you were hiding that from me…mad as I am, it's not like we're going to break up or anything. I'm stuck with you, just like you're stuck with me. That's the way it is with brothers."

If only, I thought. If only.

TWELVE

"Oh, now I see where all the confusion happened," said the lady at the front desk of the Mountain View Lodge. "*His* name isn't Victor. *Her* name is Victoria."

To me, there had not been a lot of confusion. I'd only been standing there for about thirty seconds as the lady scanned the volunteer sign-in sheet. Thirty seconds of admiring how solidly she'd sculpted the bright-red strands of her hair into something that withstood the breeze coming from a fan behind her desk. That same fan had provided me with a whiff of the hairspray responsible for that sculpture.

"Victoria?" I repeated.

"Victoria," she said. "I don't make mistakes about this sort of thing."

Implying, of course, that I did, and also that I was the source of the confusion in her normally ordered life. Anybody who had so thoroughly defeated gravity with that hairdo was a force, so I meekly accepted the scolding.

I wasn't sure what was happening. Had Victor put on a dress and a wig? Only way to find out was to go looking.

"I must have misheard the message from the foundation," I said. I shifted and felt the pain in my stomach wall from the bruise that was starting to yellow around the edges. "My apologies. If you could tell me where to find *Victoria*, I'd appreciate that."

Happily, she must have misinterpreted my wince.

"Well," she said, "the Wyatt Foundation does a great deal for these seniors, so let's not give it any more worry."

The Wyatt Foundation had so much money it employed two full-time staff to screen all the applications for charitable funding. A cynic might also note that the tax benefits were equally substantial. All I knew was that the Wyatt name made it easy to get things done, including placing volunteers for community service. As for the pre-probation judgment that Victor Lang had received by registered mail, that was sheer fiction, courtesy of Bentley's superior hacking skills. Victor had promised to do community service, but I wanted him to be scared of stepping out of line again.

"Victoria will be down the hall and to the right," Hairspray told me. "Exactly where requested. The Wyatt Courtyard Atrium. You'll notice the thank-you plaque is prominently displayed."

I let the breeze of the fan push me in the direction indicated.

When I rounded the corner, I saw the silhouette of a girl maybe a year or two younger than I standing near a number of huge windows. The sunshine directly in my eyes made it difficult to see details.

I did, however, notice four elderly men alongside the windows. One held a bottle of glass cleaner, and one held paper towels. The other two leaned on walkers.

Bottle Guy was misting the window, and Paper Towel Guy was mopping up the mist behind him. They were intent on their jobs and didn't notice my approach.

"Missed a spot," the man in the walker on the right cackled. "Right where Herb sneezed. How blind are you?"

"Rumors must be true," Bottle Guy said without a beat. "You did pee your bed this morning, didn't you?"

The other walker guy cackled too. "At least he remembers where it is."

Old-geezer jokes. Not even funny old-geezer jokes. Socially acceptable to make if you're one of the aged, but I was willing to bet the cackling would stop if I jumped in and made one myself.

"Herb," the girl said, "you just ignore those teasers. I think you're doing a wonderful job."

Bottle Guy beamed, showing a huge tray of false teeth.

Ah, now I understood. Victor had not even bothered to show up. He had somehow got Jennie, his older sister, aka Victoria, to take his place.

"Victoria?" I said. "A word?"

You used phrases like "a word" when you were young and trying to project unearned authority. Add to that a navy-blue suit tailored for you on Savile Row in London. The silk tie that complemented it was worth the price of a dinner for four at a high-end restaurant.

Suit-and-tie was good when representing the Wyatt Foundation, and

I would get double use out of it at my meeting the next day.

Jennie Lang looked my way, assessing me with a quick up-and-down flick of her eyes.

"Of course," she said, giving me a flirty smile. "A word."

She turned to her four admirers. "Gentlemen, looks like the fun and games are over for me. But keep going. I love, love, love how well you've cleaned those windows."

"Me next," Walker Guy One said. He tottered as he reached out for the spray bottle.

"Just don't sneeze," Walker Guy Two said. "Who wants to wipe that stuff off the glass?"

Jennie took a couple of steps my way. I could see why the men had lined up to take over her job.

She flaunted her classic hourglass shape with skin-tight jeans and a stretchy sleeveless shirt.

"So," she said to me, "did you lose a bet?"

I frowned.

"Seriously. A suit and tie? What are you, Junior Wall Street?"

"Wyatt Foundation supervisor," I said. "First thing I need to know is your real name and why you are here instead of Victor Lang. As I understand it, his pre-probation statement requires a minimum five hours a week of community service."

"About that," she said. "Let's find someplace private to talk. We need to get that appealed. And I bet you'd love to help me, wouldn't you?"

THIRTEEN

"So this Wyatt Foundation," Jennie said. "What's the deal?"

We'd moved to a corner of the large atrium. Less sunshine. Less squinting.

"Deal?"

"It seems like Super Geek found money at the foundation to pay for spray-paint damages. I sure didn't apply for the funding. Neither did my brother. Super Geek took over."

"Super Geek?" I said, pretending I had no clue about my alter ego. Sure, I was a bit of a grouch about being part of a team known as Retribution, but I had to admit there was something fun about playing different roles in different situations. Or maybe we all did, one way or another, and this was just an elevated version.

"How else would you describe some nerdy-looking dude who takes out three football players?" she asked in return. "My brother said it happened so quickly it was hard to follow the action. It sounded like the geeky guy gave a quick flex of muscles, and then three of them were out. And he was smaller than any of them."

"I'm unaware of any of this," I said. "I just work for the foundation. My paperwork indicates that someone made an application for funds to be applied against a vandalism incident. One condition of successful funding was that the person responsible for the vandalism serve time in community service. I'm going by memory, because the file isn't in front of me, but I believe it was a Victor Lung. You do not appear to be Victor Lung."

"Lang," she said. "Victor *Lang*. My question is, how do you manage to walk? I mean, the way you talk, it's like you have some kind of pole inserted up your—"

"You do not appear to be Victor Lang," I said. "This is a serious abrogation of the funding conditions."

"Abrogation? You lost me there."

"Dereliction," I said. Wow, it was fun talking like a suit. Private-school education has its advantages, I suppose.

"Still lost. Dereliction?"

"Promises were made that haven't been kept."

"That I can understand. So how about from here on in, you stick to real words, Junior Wall Street."

"I will do my best to comply," I said.

She leaned forward, put a hand on each side of my face and, before I could pull away, planted a deep kiss on my lips.

My flustered reaction as I pushed away was not acting in any sense. The DNA results flashed before my eyes.

She leaned back and studied me with satisfaction. "Just checking to see if you're human. Seems you are."

I stood. I walked a tight circle. I returned.

"You are not Victor Lang," I said. "I need to know why you are here instead of Victor."

"I'm Jennie. Victor is my little brother," she said, still smirking. "And you might want to wipe away some of my lipstick before you go to your next appointment."

"Your brother," I said, "needs to be accountable for his vandalism. That was a crucial part of the foundation's decision to pay for the damages."

"My dad left my mom because she had an affair," Jennie said. "Ever since then, our family—me, my mom and my brothers—has been a bit messed up. Victor needs protecting, and I'm happy to help him."

"You said *brothers*. What about the other one?"

"Good riddance to him," she said. "I'm not going into details."

I tamped down the emotions her answer caused me to feel.

"Victor," I answered, staying focused, "needs to understand that actions have consequences."

"Easy for you to say, JWS," she said.

JWS? Right. Junior Wall Street.

"I'm not about to start explaining myself or my family to you," she continued. "I'm going to head back to the windows and supervise the task I was given as part of this community-service thing."

"I notice you aren't doing the work."

"Yeah, but it's probably the highlight of those old guys' week, if not their month. I'm doing them a favor."

"Victor needs to be here doing this work as agreed."

"Well, he won't be," said Jennie. "If you don't like it, sue me."

With that, she marched back toward Herb and his three friends.

The grins on their faces at her arrival told me that yes, it probably was the highlight of their week.

Being kissed full on the lips by my sister, however, had not been any kind of highlight for me.

FOURTEEN

A scam is only as good as the believability of the lie that goes with the scam and the greediness of the person on the other end. Those aren't my words, by the way. They're Jo's. With forgeries, the same rules apply.

Jo's skills with paint and brush meant she could replicate the *Mona Lisa* so perfectly that even side by side with the original it would be impossible to tell them apart. Selling the painting, however, would have to start with a lie. For example: The one in the museum in France is a fake because it was successfully switched out years ago. The officials in the museum know this but have to keep it a secret or the French government's reputation would be destroyed. The real one was recently stolen from the Mafia crime boss who arranged for the switch, and here it is. I'm desperate for money but can't ask a lot for it, because it's too dangerous for me to be connected to this theft. I'm selling it to you for a fraction of what the painting is worth, and you're going to need to keep it a secret from the world. But you'll have the satisfaction of knowing that you have the real thing, painted by da Vinci himself.

Would you buy that story?

Probably not. Unless you were the type of person who just had to have more than everyone else and were always on the lookout for the next great thing for impressing others.

I was sitting across a lunch table from a corporate secretary named Amanda Hill. My job today was to convince her that the slip of greenish-blue paper folded inside the jacket pocket of my suit was an authentic money order for $25,000. It was not. Artwork courtesy of a certain talented forger I know.

I had been successful so far. My suit and tie added five or six years and made me look like a young and hungry corporate recruiter.

When the timing was right, I pulled the money order out of my jacket, unfolded it and slid it across the table.

Amanda glanced at the numbers, then stared at the numbers, then lifted her eyes to mine.

"That's a big signing bonus," she said.

"It is indeed. However, at this point I have to confess that pretty much our entire lunch conversation until now has been a lie," I said. "I'm not here to recruit you for another corporation."

Best way to sell a lie, Jo maintained, was to admit to a smaller lie. There was a good reason I was nervous around her.

I watched Amanda's face closely and saw the flicker of understanding that I was waiting for.

A few days earlier, Bentley had phished Amanda Hill via email and learned a couple of crucial things. The first was her log-in password for Facebook, and the second was that Amanda, like most people, was lazy about passwords. She used the same one for nearly everything she did, including online banking. Bentley was quickly able to determine that she had deposited $12,500 into her account about two weeks earlier and then another $12,500 two days after that.

Deanna Steele had provided us with her father's calendar, and we'd cross-checked the date of the second deposit. It was the day after Martin Steele had been at an off-site corporate event at a resort. The resort pool matched the one in the photos.

I was here to check out a theory we had about that day.

"I can't tell you who sent me here," I continued, "because I don't know who it is. I just know that I'm supposed to ask you if you would be willing to do it again. If the answer is yes, this money order is yours."

We figured that if Amanda Hill had been paid to set up Deanna Steele's father, it was unlikely she knew the identity of the blackmailer. She'd probably received half up front and half after completing her job.

"I don't know if that will be possible," Amanda answered.

I reached across the table and slid the fake money order back toward me.

"It's not that I won't try," she said quickly, eyes on the money order. "What I meant was, Martin was really mad at me when I kissed him at the pool. He won't be as easy to trick next time around."

Spy gadgets are easy to purchase and so effective. On the table were the journal and pen I'd used to make pretend notes as we discussed her possible job offer over lunch. The pen was recording our entire conversation. Deanna was going to be very happy to hear what Amanda had just said.

"If you can explain what you mean," I said, "I can take that back to the people who sent me."

She reached across the table and, with perfectly manicured fingers, slid the money order back in her direction.

"What I mean is," she said, "if your people were smart enough to figure out how to set Martin up the first time, all they need to do is come back with a good plan the second time. It was easy enough to lean over and kiss him when he wasn't expecting it. But now his guard is up. I'll do whatever they want, but they need to know that I almost lost my job."

She lifted the slip of paper, folded it and tucked it into her purse.

"So tell your people that I'll take this," she said. "And another one for double.

That should cover me when I actually lose my job for trying to make him look like more than my boss."

"Of course," I said. "I'll tell them that."

I didn't know what was going to be more satisfying: telling Deanna that her father had not been having an affair with his secretary, or seeing the expression on Amanda's face when she tried to deposit that fake money order.

FIFTEEN

I call it my street apartment. It's in the East Hastings area. If you live in Vancouver, you know that "East Hastings" is a catchall phrase for drug addicts, discarded needles and the broken shells of homeless people pushing shopping carts loaded with all their possessions.

For all its flaws, this concentrated area of poverty has the vibrancy that comes with desperation for life. In the weeks after my father was arrested, I found a way to survive there by playing street chess. Sure, being rich has some benefits, but there's nothing like trying to survive from day to day—or even hour to hour—to heighten all your senses.

I like returning to that life so I kept the lease for the apartment even after moving back to the Batcave to be close to Bentley. The interior has walls of cracked paint, carpet with stains whose origins are best left unexplored and light fixtures dotted with dead insects. With a pullout couch and a bathroom the size of a phone booth, it's perfect.

To me, this grungy studio apartment on the Downtown Eastside represents freedom.

But I'm careful. Every time I leave, I prop a matchstick against the bottom of the door so I will know if anyone has broken in.

This was evening two after my meeting with Amanda Hill. Enough time for the bait to have been taken. I made my way to the apartment. As I prepared to unlock the door, I checked for the matchstick.

It was no longer propped in place.

Along with a small burst of adrenaline, I felt sadness. The peace and solitude I cherished in my little sanctuary was gone already.

I pushed the door open and resisted the temptation to look around. There were no obvious signs of a break-in. This was not your typical East Hastings crash-and-grab. Anyone with the motivation and the technology skills to trace me to this apartment was someone who would likely leave behind a spy camera. I had to assume that I would be under surveillance from the moment I stepped inside.

My first move was to go to the refrigerator and pull out a bag of carrots. I chomped away for a few minutes, then drank some water straight from the tap. I didn't want to look like I was in a hurry to get to my computer.

When I finally sat down in front of it, I opened up a video chat and clicked on Deanna Steele's email address.

When she answered, I noticed a Teenage Mutant Ninja Turtles poster behind her.

"How are you and Donatello doing?" I asked.

She caught the reference immediately and flashed me a big grin.

It looked good on her.

"Let me get right to it," I said. "It worked. Amanda took the money."

Deanna knew what this meant right away. Her father had been set up.

I'd expected her to look pleased. What I got, however, was much more alarming. Her face crumpled as tears dropped down her cheeks. She sobbed soundlessly. I didn't interrupt.

"Thank you," she finally said. "I felt like I'd lost my father. You gave him back to me."

Wow. That felt good. Aware that I was probably being watched, though, I played it cool.

"Now what we have to do is make sure nothing gets in the way of the corporate merger," I said. "You passed along your father's passwords to the blackmailer, right?"

"Yes, but if the software backdoor didn't work," she said, "I've just destroyed his career."

"I promise you," I said. "Everything is perfect. The log-in password will take them to a mirror of your father's hard drive with all the fake information we put in it."

"And the real information?"

I held up a small keychain and the dangling USB stick. "It's with me twenty-four/seven. No way are we trusting it anywhere in the Cloud. Any hacker as good as my brother and me would find a way to get there from your father's computer. And we're assuming the blackmailer has hired the best."

"Really," she said. "How can I ever thank you?"

"Let's wait until the blackmailer takes the bait," I said. "It will probably happen tonight, so I'm meeting with a lawyer to pull together the information we need. By noon the cops should be involved, and after that we can celebrate."

"I like the sound of that," she said. Her big smile was back.

"Cool," I said. "And, um, thought I'd ask if you might want to meet me somewhere."

I gave her the name and address of the boxing gym.

"To watch you work out?" She laughed. "Nice try. Muscles don't impress me."

"I'll be there late," I said, "in case you change your mind. I'll leave the back door unlocked."

She laughed again and waved goodbye. I did the same and ended our connection.

The conversation had gone as well as I had expected. Deanna deserved an Oscar for it.

And now the clock was ticking for the blackmailer.

SIXTEEN

Snap and flow, I repeated to myself. *Snap and flow.*

I was the last one of the night, alone in the gym, facing the heavy bag in one of the corners.

Billy, the owner, was okay with my staying late. He'd made a second set of keys for me and trusted me to lock up.

Technically, they were my keys.

Billy had no idea that I was the one who had purchased the building a few weeks earlier, when it looked like a rent increase might put him out of business. Six months' interest on my trust fund had been more than enough to buy the building. As far as he knew, the landlord had sold the building to some conglomerate that would develop the property in a few years. Until further notice he was welcome to stay put, at a very reasonable rate.

Snap and flow.

To me, the heavy bag, more than the speed bag, is the symbol of boxing. Dinging the speed bag over and over takes a coordination that is mesmerizing for spectators.

But the heavy bag—so wide you could circle your arms around it, and weighing half of your body weight—is where your grit and determination are built. How you handle the heavy bag makes the difference between slamming to the ring floor with buckled knees or having the ref raise your hand in victory.

As long as you don't get lazy with it.

The temptation is to push your punches through it. The feeling of power you get by doing that is an illusion. You need to snap your punches, letting the impact of the bag bounce your fist back. Learn how to do this right, and you'll punch harder and faster with less energy expended. And you need all the energy you can get. If you've ever been in a fight, you learn how much the adrenaline saps the energy from you.

Snap and flow.

It's not about the punches you throw but *how* you throw them in combinations as you move around the bag. If you set your feet and throw the hardest punch possible, you are not flowing. Try that against a good boxer and watch your fist slip past the target. Then feel the return punch catch you square because your feet are immobile.

Snap and flow. Snap and flow.

I hit the heavy bag. *RAT-A-TAT-TAT* punches at 50 to 70 percent power, never pausing more than three seconds between combinations.

It is far more physically demanding than hitting a speed bag. I'd been at it for ten minutes, and sweat poured from my skin, sending splatters of moisture at every impact.

Snap and flow. Snap and flow.

I kept my eyes on the exact spot I wanted to hit each time. I pretended I was trying to hit a quarter glued in that position. Too many boxers let their eyes wander around the gym as they hit. This is a complacency that will hurt you in the ring.

Snap and flow. Snap and flow.

I kept exactly within arm's reach of the bag. I didn't want to be in the ring against someone who always managed to be out of my reach and who always managed to sense when I'd moved within his reach. Without distance awareness, all the punches I threw would be meaningless once the bell rang.

Snap and flow. Snap and flow.

I was in my intense little world, my focus totally on the sound of my gloves against the bag.

Snap and flow. Snap and flow.

Then something interrupted my focus.

The sound of a single person clapping.

I looked past the bag and saw the source of that sound.

Jennie Lang. Smirking at me. And clapping in a manner that was clearly sarcastic.

I stopped punching and wiped my forearm across my forehead to keep the sweat from dripping into my eyes.

"Surprised?" she said. "Maybe you should think of locking the doors this late at night."

I was surprised. I said nothing. I was wearing a black workout shirt. It was soaked, and now that I'd stopped punching, the shirt felt as uncomfortable as the boxing gloves that kept my fingers prisoner. I wanted to keep hitting the bag.

"You Retribution guys, you like privacy, right?" she asked. "You want to be some kind of shadowy Internet group that no one knows if it's real or not."

She lifted her right hand. The gym was poorly lit because I had turned down most of the lights. But I could make out that she was holding up a cell phone.

"You're not that smart," she said. "At the seniors' center? You believed me when I said I was going back to supervising the window cleaning. Hardly. I ducked out and made it to my car before you could leave. I followed you home after your lunch with the chick with too much makeup. Seriously, you can do better than that. Victor and I talked about what to do. So tonight I follwed you again and la-dee-da, here we are."

Home. I had to give it thought. After lunch with Amanda Hill, I'd gone to...

the grungy apartment. Not the mansion. That was a good thing. To her, then, I was Jace Sanders, the name I used on the apartment lease and the name I used at the gym.

"Junior Wall Street," she sneered. "Living in a dump like that? How pitiful, putting on that suit and pretending you're some rich dude."

She took a step toward me, holding the phone at eye level. Short of assaulting her to take it away, I didn't know what to do.

"Jace Sanders," she said. "I know your name. I know where you live. I know where you work out. And I've got this recorded. Your secrets are no longer secret."

It would have been worse—much worse—if she knew I was a Wyatt from the Wyatt Foundation. But this was bad enough. If she posted something on YouTube and it got any kind of traction, sooner or later someone would make the link.

But that wasn't the very worst part. There was a reason I'd been hitting the heavy bag so late this evening. And there was a reason I hadn't locked the doors for my workout.

"Look," I said. "Could we talk about this tomorrow?"

"No," she answered. "Tomorrow you might be in a position to hurt me."

"And I'm not right now?"

"No," she said. "You're not."

That's when a noose dropped over my head and tightened on my throat like a ring of fire.

SEVENTEEN

"On your knees," Victor Lang said from behind me.

I was trying to understand what had just happened. Obviously the delay was too much for him, because the noose tightened and twisted.

I gagged.

"On your knees," Victor repeated.

I dropped. I was still wearing my boxing gloves. I couldn't use my fingers to claw at the noose. Even if I could, I doubted it would help.

Still, I had to try. I brought my gloves to my mouth and used my teeth to snap the Velcro loose on the right glove.

"Stop right there," Victor said. The noose tightened again, so tight this time it cut off my gag.

"Ease off," Jennie told her brother. "You don't want to kill him."

"Maybe I do," Victor said. But the pressure eased. I could breathe again. It didn't help the pain of my knees pressed against the floor.

"Impressed?" Jennie asked. "We decided on an animal snare. Because that's what you are. An animal."

Now, at least, I could picture the situation. Victor was holding an aluminum pole with a noose at the end. While they talked, I started working my right glove loose again. My only chance was to get my fingers free, maybe try to spin and jerk the pole out of his hands.

"Animal?" I said. I wanted to keep the conversation going, distract her.

"You've bullied my brother from the beginning."

"*I've* bullied *him?*" I snorted. "Do you have any idea what he does to the younger—"

I gagged again as Victor jerked on the noose.

"Not so nice when I'm the one in control," he said, "is it?"

He was right. It wasn't so nice.

"Here's the deal," Jennie said. "Leave us alone. Completely. Or I will put your real identity out there. Got it?"

I thought about the implications. She must have taken my silence as resistance to her demand.

"Victor wants to strangle you and bury your body," Jennie told me. "Just so you understand, I believe that's easily done. We could march you out of here, put you in my car, strangle you in the backseat, drive somewhere into the mountains and dig a hole deep enough to hide the evidence. Even if someone found your body, who would ever link you to me and Victor?"

At first that sounded ridiculous. But then I realized it wasn't that impossible to carry out. An animal snare allowed someone to control huge dogs. If I didn't walk along with the noose, they'd strangle me here in the gym and just drag my body to their car.

As if reading my thoughts, Victor jerked the noose again.

"I told Victor we didn't need to go that far," Jennie said. "We just had to convince you to stay out of our lives."

"Victor," I said with gritted teeth, "was the one to invite me into your life."

"Yeah, about that," Jennie said. "I don't think it was a coincidence that Victor received an anonymous email telling him about Team Retribution and strongly suggesting he reach out to them."

My muscles were cooling, and I shivered.

Jennie's eyes gleamed with triumph. "Thought so," she said. "It was you."

Yeah. It was.

"Did someone else ask you to step in to bother us?" she asked. "Is that how Retribution got into our lives?"

I imagined how it might sound, telling her that I was her older brother. And that I was trying to find a way to help their family. *My* family. But how do you tell someone that everything they know to be true just isn't?

"Answer," she said, sudden fury in her voice.

"I sent the email because of your missing brother," I said. This, at least, was absolutely true. That I meant me as well as Elias when I said *missing brother* was something I still didn't know if I should ever reveal.

"Elias?" she said.

I nodded.

"Where is he?"

Before I could think of an answer that might make her happy, two large men walked out of the shadows and directly toward us.

Each carried a baseball bat.

EIGHTEEN

I was on my knees. Victor could see clearly over my head.

"Jen!" he said. "Behind you."

She turned her head, and at the sight of the large men she took an involuntary step toward me.

It was an intimidating sight. Both wore black sneakers, black jeans and black sweatshirts. The sweatshirts were stretched by massive chest and arm muscles.

Both also wore black masks.

The muscles and size I didn't like so much, but I was relieved to see them wearing masks. If they didn't want to be identified, it meant they intended to leave witnesses alive.

As to whether the witnesses would be undamaged by those bats, I had no answer.

I did know that what made the men more frightening was that neither slapped the bats against their palms. Barking dogs are less frightening than, say, silent rottweilers advancing with intent in their eyes.

Jennie moved quickly behind me. The noose kept me from moving my head, but I could imagine her standing shoulder to shoulder with Victor.

"Weird party," the first guy said, stopping three steps away from us. "Time to break it up."

"Any closer and we snap the noose so tight it takes his head off," Jennie said.

Nice to have a sister so concerned about my health.

"Then we'll be searching a dead body instead of a living body," the second guy said. "Makes no difference to us. As for you, I'd say the video surveillance will make for a nice long prison term."

"Video…" Jennie's voice echoed uncertainty.

Convenient that I hadn't brought it up as a subject for discussion. But yeah, there were small cameras in discreet places. While a boxing gym isn't the kind of target that a jewelry store might be, insurance companies give better rates if you have surveillance in place. As the new owner of the building, I'd had cameras installed not too long ago.

"We really don't care what you're doing to him or why," the first guy said. "Trust me on this. All we want is the USB stick."

The second guy stepped closer. He extended the baseball bat and tapped my left cheekbone with the end of it.

"Well, princess," he said. "Where is it?"

"Victor," I said. My hands were in front of me. My right glove dangled from my fingertips. All I had to do was straighten my fingers and it would fall. "Now would be a good time to remove the snare."

"I'd rather watch them hurt you," Victor said.

If I hadn't allowed myself to believe it before, I knew it now. The kid was seriously messed up when it came to any kind of moral code.

The second guy tapped my other cheekbone with the end of his bat.

"And now would be a good time to tell me where the USB stick is," he repeated. "Last chance."

"It's in my boxing glove," I said. I flicked the fingers of my right hand, and the glove bounced across the floor.

The first guy took a quick step. Keeping his bat in his right hand, he used his left hand to grab the glove and shake it upside down.

The USB stick, in a small ziplock bag to protect it from my sweat, tumbled to the floor.

He scooped it up and slid it into his front pocket.

"Sorry, princess," the second guy said, tapping my cheekbone one more time. "Apparently you've been a pain. We have instructions to hurt you in return."

"Victor," I said. "Need help here."

Victor shifted his voice, and I knew it was directed at the men in masks. "You don't need to hurt us, right?"

"You're not part of this," the first guy answered.

"Victor," I said. "Remember when I kept five guys from beating on you? Drop the snare. That's all I need."

"I also remember you trying to make me do community service," he answered. "Like I'm some kind of project of yours."

Jennie said to me, "They hurt you bad enough, Victor and I will have time to find out where the video surveillance is stored, and we can erase it."

"Nice to have friends," the first guy said. He turned to his partner. "Let's get this done."

The guy in front of me raised the baseball bat. "Nothing personal," he said.

"Same in return," I told him. "You guys started this. I'm happy to escalate it."

"What?" he asked.

I answered with one word. I spoke it clearly and loudly. "Retribution."

All the lights went out.

NINETEEN

Fire codes demand that when the power goes out in a commercial building, emergency lights powered by battery automatically go on. I knew this from the paperwork I'd had to go through when buying the property.

These lights did not kick in. The interior of the building was the black of a night sky without stars. Given time for my eyes to adjust, I might have been able to find an outline, but whatever light seeped into this part of the building from the windows at the front was, at this point, useless.

"Nobody move," growled one of the two thugs in the dark.

Too late.

I'd already reached over my shoulder with my gloveless right hand to grab the end of the pole. I yanked it from Victor's grasp. Immediately the noose slackened around my neck. He yelped. I ignored that.

I stood. I pulled the noose over my head and dropped the pole. I ripped the Velcro from my other glove and popped it off.

This might have taken three or four seconds.

Then I heard a sound I'd been expecting.

A scream.

In the total darkness it was as eerie as if this were a horror movie. Especially when the second—and equally high-pitched—scream followed a heartbeat later.

It wasn't from Victor or Jennie. They were behind me.

It came from the guys with the baseball bats. Those bats clattered on the floor as each of the screams died. Then a second set of screams.

I knew what was happening to them, but they didn't.

Cattle prods. Set at medium voltage. Long handheld sticks with two points, powered by battery. Not deadly, but on contact enough to jolt a thousand-pound animal into a spasm of movement. Before buying the cattle prods, I'd watched a couple of YouTube videos where idiots tried them on each other.

Another set of screams.

I could picture each of the two large men flailing in the darkness. How long would it take for them to realize their best option was to try to run?

I didn't get a chance to find out.

From behind me came bright light, all the more piercing because of the contrast to the sheer black.

The first result was to illuminate what had been happening. It caught Raven and Jo, dressed in black and each holding a cattle prod, about to strike again.

But both of them had stumbled, disoriented.

That was because of the second result.

Raven and Jo each wore a pair of helmet-mounted night-vision goggles, NVGs, standard military issue, retail price well over four thousand dollars. They were able to produce images in near total darkness, converting minimal light and near infrared into green images for the viewer.

I knew the price because I'd purchased them the day before. I knew they worked and how they worked because Raven and Jo and I had tested them in the gym with all the lights out. It was weird, seeing a person's body displayed all in green, but effective.

The plan had been perfect. Set myself up alone in the gym late at night with the door open, like a tethered goat placed in the jungle to attract a tiger. Call out for help with our code word. Plunge the gym into darkness. And let Jo and Raven attack at their leisure.

The key word was *had*. As in, the plan *had* been perfect. Until Jennie turned on her phone's flashlight.

The NVGs had been set to maximum intensity. Which meant Jennie's light had blinded Raven and Jo with such impact that it might be minutes before they could see normally again.

I would have turned to snatch the device from Jennie, but the two large men recovered as quickly as cats landing on their feet.

One punched Raven in the gut. The other clouted Jo across the helmet. They'd already been disoriented, and this attack was enough to knock them both to the floor.

One of the men reached for a bat. The other lifted a foot to kick.

Grabbing the device from Jennie was no longer an option. I leapt forward, twisting and turning as I threw my right elbow into the jaw of the one about to kick Jo. He grunted and staggered.

The other grabbed at my arm. I spun loose and threw a punch into his gut.

Snap and flow.

It was like hitting the heavy bag, and he staggered back from the impact.

This was not good.

The elbow to the jaw should have knocked the first guy onto the floor. The punch to the gut should have doubled over the second guy to his knees.

These guys could take some serious punishment. I needed to keep moving and extend the fight until they exhausted themselves. My only chance to was use my better fitness and mobility to my advantage. If either of them managed to latch on to me, I was dead. Metaphorically for sure and maybe literally if they started landing big punches or picked up the baseball bats.

Snap and flow.

What made this surreal was the single light source that seemed to etch everything into black and white.

"Guys," I told them between gulping deep breaths. "We've got two minutes to finish this. My friends here triggered a 9-1-1 call when they shut down the lights. We're expecting the cops at any time. That was the plan."

I danced in close to the guy I'd popped on the jaw. I ducked and faked a punch with my right hand, and I snapped a punch into his gut with the left. I didn't want to hit any part of his skull. Not with an unprotected fist.

I danced back as he grunted.

Again, I was impressed by his ability to take punishment.

I caught some movement at my left. I weaved out of the way of a roundhouse from the second guy. He was fast.

Snap and flow.

I was trying to find my rhythm, trying

to buy time for Raven and Jo, who were still on the floor.

That's when a noose settled over my head again.

"Gotcha!" Victor said.

Really? I thought. Really?

My final conscious thought ended a heartbeat later as another roundhouse found its target.

Side of my skull.

I didn't even see the floor on my way down.

TWENTY

I woke to a jolt of electricity in my brain. I flailed, thinking *cattle prod*.

"Easy, Hulk," Jo said.

I blinked a few times. I saw that I had been propped up in a chair along one of the walls of the gym.

I saw that Jo was holding a small torn packet below my nose.

Smelling salts. Snapping me awake like electricity.

That was the nice thing, I suppose, about getting your clock cleaned in a boxing gym. The convenience of something nearby to shock you back to consciousness.

Not so nice was the burst of ammonia in my nose that came with it.

I also saw that Raven was offering me a bag of ice.

I pressed it against the side of my head.

Wow. That had been some kind of punch.

"What about my pupils?" I said.

"Pupils?" Raven said. "Like you were teaching those guys something? That's not how I remember it."

I groaned. "If it's not too much trouble, would you mind checking the pupils of my eyes to see if they are of equal size?"

Jo leaned forward. As always, I felt a sense of unspoken tension as our eyes locked. And unspoken it would remain.

She assessed me. I took the opportunity to do the same.

"Looks normal," she said.

I gave a small nod, afraid anything bigger might hurt.

I went through a mental checklist. Temporary loss of consciousness was a definite sign of possible concussion. So that was a worry. But pupils were okay and I didn't feel pressure in my head or any dizziness. No nausea. If I were my trainer, I wouldn't let myself back in the ring. But I'd probably conclude that I likely didn't have a concussion.

I stood to check my balance. So far, so good.

Except for the two cattle prods on the floor a few steps away and the NVG helmets beside them and the emptiness of the gym. A reminder of what Jennie had caused by turning on that flashlight.

"Hey," I said. "Don't you love it when a well-executed plan ends perfectly?"

Raven said, "I wanted to snap her neck. Getting hit with the light was like being stabbed in the eyeballs."

"Can't say I liked getting knocked down," Jo said.

"Oh, I loved it," I said.

"Maybe we need to take you to Emergency," Raven said to me.

"Nope," I answered. "Now I finally understand what it's like to take a serious punch. Downside to being as good as I am in the ring, it's never happened before."

"Ha-ha," Raven said. "Clearly you are back to your normal obnoxious self."

Maybe not. I sat back in the chair. No ringing in my ears, at least. But right now I preferred sitting to standing.

Jo and Raven each dragged a chair over. They had me surrounded.

"First I'll ask the obvious," I said. "How long was I out? And then why is it that we're here and they are not?"

"Your bluff worked," Jo answered. "Telling them about the 9-1-1 call and cops on the way. Both goons took off as you were hitting the floor. At least, I think that's what happened. I was still struggling to get some vision back."

There certainly had *not* been a 9-1-1 call. Last thing we'd wanted was cops involved.

"They took the USB stick?" I asked.

Raven nodded. "None of us were in a position to take it back. It's gone."

I massaged my skull with the ice pack. "And evil sister and brother?"

While I meant those terms literally, Raven and Jo had no way of knowing this. I wasn't about to explain.

"Evil sister left a message for you," Raven said. "You do anything with the surveillance tapes and she puts out her own videos on social media."

"You know," Jo said. "Her videos that show your face and my face and Raven's face in clear view. Not a good thing for the team."

Team.

"Nice cold-war tactic," I said. "Mutually assured destruction. I'm okay with that. She leaves us alone, we leave her alone."

I had to tell them that, but then I thought about it some more. Yes. I *was* okay with that. I think I now understood that old phrase *You can lead a horse to water, but you can't make it drink*. I didn't really see how Jennie and Victor and I could ever have any sort of relationship.

"On her way out, she didn't seem too concerned about whether you'd even wake up," Raven said. "Interesting how you successfully manage to make so many females angry with you. I'd love to know the specifics of this one. Maybe start with what happened at the seniors' center she mentioned, and why she thinks you've bullied her brother. What was that about you making him a project of yours?"

The plan had been for Jo and Raven to be hiding while I waited for the blackmailer to make a move. Having Jennie and Victor show up had not been part of the plan. Nor was Jo and Raven overhearing the conversation while I had a noose around my neck.

"And the evil brother," Jo said. "It was obvious he hated you. Like, I mean *hated.* You should have seen the joy on his face while he had the noose around your neck."

Yes. I was definitely okay with not trying to be part of the lives of Jennie and Victor.

"Raven," I said. "Jo. I've never asked the two of you to trust me before. But now I am. This is something I need to work through myself. Can you give me that?"

It took a few seconds for them each to give me a nod of agreement.

"Thanks," I said. I hid from them any warmth I might have felt about the trust they had just offered me.

But it occurred to me that this was what it must be like being part of a team.

TWENTY-ONE

Speed chess on the street and twenty dollars on the line.

I was staring at the board, trying to stay focused on the two moves remaining to trap my opponent's unprotected white king and win that twenty dollars.

I didn't want to look up from the board. The dude had a monstrous pimple on the end of his nose that was so close to popping, the pressure must have been like a bee sting. How could he not be aware of it? Or did he look in the mirror and say, *Yeah, why not draw attention away from the grease stains on my shirt?*

The only difference between taking that twenty and swiping a lollipop from a toddler was that the dude across from me actually believed he had a chance of keeping his money and walking away with mine.

He hit the clock. I moved a piece and hit the clock. He wasted thirty seconds in panic, wasted another thirty seconds thinking he could actually escape, made a move, then hit the clock.

It's not that I'm good in the way chess champions are good. In hockey terms, I'm like a ten-year-old with some skills. The real chess champions are destined for the NHL.

But we humans tend to fool ourselves with inflated estimates of our abilities. The real chess players—the pros—would have wiped me off the board in minutes. But Pimple Nose hadn't even learned to tie his skates.

Add the pressure of playing against the clock. Make a move, hit the clock, force the other player into hearing the seconds count down on his end. Run out of time, lose the game.

Time and again, people who had been playing chess at home for a few years thought they knew it well enough to snap up the two twenties under a rock on the table. Those were the stakes I offered. Win, you get forty. Lose, I get twenty. But I didn't lose often, so in this touristy area I cleared a couple hundred bucks most days.

With time clicking away, I swooped in with my queen, hit the clock and announced "Checkmate." I took his twenty and let my gaze slide past his nose and over his shoulder as he gave a rueful shrug.

That's when I saw Jennie Lang, holding a Starbucks cup and threading her way down the crowded sidewalk.

"Better luck next time," I said to Pimple Nose.

He took the hint, scraped his chair back and left me alone.

I tucked the bills into my pocket and folded up the chessboard. The table was empty by the time Jennie arrived.

She set her cup on the table and set her face into a granite look of displeasure.

"We weren't clear enough last night that we want you out of our lives?" she said.

"I'm doing fine," I replied. "That last punch across the head didn't hurt at all. Thanks for asking."

"I'm only here because you said you had news about Elias."

"Thought you might want to know where he is," I said.

"That's not why I showed up."

"No?"

She lifted her cup for a quick and angry sip, then set it down again.

"I'm here to tell you one last time to stay out of our lives. Victor and I don't give a crap about Elias. He's the freaky half brother we've never liked. It took years, but Victor and I finally managed to drive him out of the house."

"Harsh."

"Not as harsh as my mom. She's always hated him too. Evidence of an affair that broke up our so-called happy family."

I tried doing the chronology. "But you and Victor were born after—"

"My father said he struggled with it for years. Not wanting to do a paternity test because he didn't want to find out. Victor was three when they split up."

I supposed the odds weren't that crazy. Plenty of husbands and wives had affairs. Except in this case, Elias had been conceived not as the result of an affair but by a different woman during the same time that Jennie's mother, Melanie, happened to have been having an affair. Since Melanie was my birth mother, did I owe her the truth?

I was messed up about this. One thing I did know for sure was that how Jennie and Victor had treated their brother, blood or not, was disgusting. They were mean and vicious people. I had no desire to be a part of their lives.

"Okay," I said.

"Okay?"

"Okay," I repeated. "I'm out of your lives."

She left the coffee cup on the table for me to throw in the trash.

TWENTY-TWO

The building was typical corporate—glass and steel on the outside, hushed lobby on the inside. I'd taken the elevator to the twenty-second floor with Deanna Steele.

"My dad's office is on the corner," she said. "Great view of Vancouver."

That, however, was not our destination. Her father had set up a meeting in a conference room. That's where two men in suits, both in their mid-twenties, were waiting for us, already seated at an oval table. They were from the marketing department—large men built like rugby players. One was blond and the other a redhead, both with close-cropped hair.

I looked for and saw flinches in their faces as I followed Deanna into the room.

"Hey," I said. "Nice to see you again. Obvious as it is to point out, you do look better in suits than in masks."

They exchanged glances, and then Red spoke. "Deanna? Not sure what this is about. We've never met this guy before."

"Baseball bats?" I said. "Boxing gym? Which of you did I tag first? Have to say, you were both in trouble until someone noosed me from behind."

Blondie pushed his chair back. "Deanna, what's going on? We're here as a favor to your father. But if you're going to waste our time—"

"My father's going to be a little busy for the next while. Police business and all that. It seems that your direct boss has been involved in corporate espionage.

And since your direct boss reports to my father, it's going to be time-consuming for everyone involved."

Both of the men sat a little more upright.

"Yeah," I said. "Turns out a certain USB stick was a bit of a setup. You know, the one you took from my boxing glove? As soon as your boss plugged it into his computer, your game was over."

A scam is only as good as the believability of the lie that goes with the scam and the greediness of the person on the other end.

To find the blackmailer's identity, Bentley had needed a backdoor into the blackmailer's computer. He'd installed a spy program to automatically download whenever the USB stick was inserted into a computer. Once we had the IP address, getting the physical address would be easy.

But to sell the blackmailer the lie, we'd needed to make it look like the USB stick had value. During a second conversation with Deanna we made it clear she and I didn't know the computer had been hacked. That conversation had sent these guys straight to the boxing gym late at night to steal the USB stick.

But if they'd taken it from me too easily, the blackmailer might have been suspicious. Our plan had been to make it look like a trap by springing Jo and Raven on them, and then letting them fight their way out. While Victor thought he was doing them a favor by noosing me, it had actually sold the lie completely.

"Also," Deanna said, "turns out your boss had no problem ratting you guys out."

Red stood and growled at me. He shrugged off his suit jacket. "Going to pound you into the ground. Should have taken you down when I had the chance."

That was all we needed.

I stood. "Would love to dance, really. But didn't it occur to you that Deanna was mic'ed and someone would monitor this conversation? Take it away, Deanna."

"Retribution," she said, loudly and clearly.

As a code word, I thought it had merit.

Two seconds later, three armed police officers knocked on the conference room door.

TWENTY-THREE

"Hoping we can talk," I said to Bentley. "Just to warn you, this is going to be a serious one."

He lifted his head from the computer and swiveled his chair away from his desk.

"Nice to meet the author of *Over the Cliff*," he said.

Book titles again. *Over the Cliff*. Written by Hugo First.

As in, this was going to be my conversation to lead. My smile should have been bigger, but it had taken me a lot of emotional strength to, first, decide it was time for the conversation and, second, initiate it.

"*The Cat's Revenge*," I said, settling into a soft chair in the corner of the room.

"By Claude Bottom," he answered. "And how about *Modern Giants*?"

"Don't know that author," I said.

"Hugh."

I played along. "Hugh?"

"Mungous."

"Nice," I said.

He smiled at me. I tried to smile back.

I said, "This is about Elias Lang."

"Great guy," Bentley said. "I think you'll like him."

"Huh?" I couldn't help but lean forward.

"After my last conversation with you, I decided I was wrong. I did want to meet him. We've been Skyping every day since. He says I'd really enjoy Ecuador and the community he's in. Nobody there treats people like us as freaks."

"Skyping."

"A software program? Allows people to have live video conversations, computer to computer or device to device or device to computer. Old technology, actually. I'm surprised you're not aware of it."

"Yeah yeah," I said. "You've been Skyping with Elias Lang. I get the Skype part. But not the having conversations with him."

Bentley shook his head and gave me a look of mock sadness. "Remember one of my favorite books? *Advanced Thinking*? I'm that author."

I nodded. *Advanced Thinking* by Smart E. Pants.

"You didn't think I'd look more closely into this after I found out you and Elias shared the same birthday and were born in the same hospital? Didn't think I'd wonder why the report given to you by your hired private investigator answered the query as to whether Melanie Lang carried mutated GHR genes?"

Only parents with mutated GHR genes could have a baby with dwarfism.

"You hacked the private investigator's computer?" I said.

"Child's play," Bentley said. "I think there's a bigger issue here. We've got another brother, and you've known it for a while. That's where this serious conversation was going, right?"

"I...uh..."

"Let me speak frankly," Bentley said. "Sometimes your protective-older-brother routine gets old. You make presumptive decisions without giving the people involved a say in the matter."

"I...uh..."

"How did it work out, stepping in to fix Victor's life because you saw him as another younger brother who needed help?"

"Victor?"

Bentley grinned. "Jo and Raven told me about the weird conversation they overheard while you were fighting at the gym. By the way, the school counselors have already made notations that he is likely a genuine sociopath. It's going to be tough to make any progress there."

"The gym?" I didn't feel smart, echoing Bentley each time.

"The same gym that you purchased to protect Billy. Without giving him a chance to ask if he wanted protecting. I'm thinking that therapy for this hero complex of yours might not be a bad idea."

It wasn't.

"I might be learning some good lessons," I said. "Could save me money on therapy."

"You've earned some redemption by deciding to let me in on Elias," Bentley said. "I've been waiting for this conversation, but it was on you to come to me."

"Let me get this straight. You and Elias, you've been talking."

"Any idea how amazing it is for me

to spend time with him? All his life the guy's felt so alone and isolated and been treated like dog poop by his entire family, everyone thinking he was proof his mom had had an affair and blaming him for wrecking the marriage."

"Cool," I said as neutrally as possible. "I can see how the two of you would click."

"We click," Bentley said. "Definitely."

I looked away.

When I looked back, I saw that Bentley had stopped smiling, and tears were trickling down his cheeks. "Jace, you're not going to stop being my brother just because our blood types don't indicate we have the same mother and father."

That was a fear I hadn't even been able to admit to myself. But he'd nailed it.

"I'm not losing a brother," Bentley added. "I'm gaining one. Now there are three of us."

I found myself blinking back tears. "Hugo First wrote another book. Don't know if you've read it."

"Do tell," Bentley said, wiping his face with his left forearm.

"*The Secret Life of Lemmings*," I answered.

It took him a moment. Then he burst into the deep laughter I'd loved hearing when he was younger. When he snuck into my bedroom late at night because he was scared or lonely.

I didn't know if there was a sound in the world I liked more than that.

ACKNOWLEDGMENTS

Judith Graves and Natasha Deen—thanks for allowing me into the lives of your characters. You've made Team Retribution such an amazing ride.